Acting Edition

Truth Be Told

by William Cameron

FOR PRODUCTION INQUIRIES

UNITED STATES AND CANADA
info@concordtheatricals.com
1-866-979-0447

UNITED KINGDOM AND EUROPE
licensing@concordtheatricals.co.uk
020-7054-7298

Each title is subject to availability from Concord Theatricals Corp., depending upon country of performance. Please be aware that *TRUTH BE TOLD* may not be licensed by Concord Theatricals Corp. in your territory. Professional and amateur producers should contact the nearest Concord Theatricals Corp. office or licensing partner to verify availability.

No one shall make any changes in this title(s) for the purpose of production. No part of this book may be reproduced, stored in a retrieval system, scanned, uploaded, or transmitted in any form, by any means, now known or yet to be invented, including mechanical, electronic, digital, photocopying, recording, videotaping, or otherwise, without the prior written permission of the publisher. No one shall share this title(s), or any part of this title(s), through any social media or file hosting websites.

For all inquiries regarding motion picture, television, online/digital and other media rights, please contact Concord Theatricals Corp.

MUSIC AND THIRD-PARTY MATERIALS USE NOTE

Licensees are solely responsible for obtaining formal written permission from copyright owners to use copyrighted music and/or other copyrighted third-party materials (e.g. artworks, logos) in the performance of this play and are strongly cautioned to do so. If no such permission is obtained by the licensee, then the licensee must use only original music and materials that the licensee owns and controls. Licensees are solely responsible and liable for clearances of all third-party copyrighted materials, including without limitation music, and shall indemnify the copyright owners of the play(s) and their licensing agent, Concord Theatricals Corp., against any costs, expenses, losses and liabilities arising from the use of such copyrighted third-party materials by licensees. For music, please contact the appropriate music licensing authority in your territory for the rights to any incidental music.

IMPORTANT BILLING AND CREDIT REQUIREMENTS

If you have obtained performance rights to this title, please refer to your licensing agreement for important billing and credit requirements.

TRUTH BE TOLD was first produced by the Curious Theatre Company in Denver, Colorado, in January 2024. The performance was directed by Christy Montour-Larson, with sets by Caitlin Ayer, costumes by Janice Benning Lacek, wig design by Richard Krammes, lighting design by Colin D. Young, sound design by Jason Ducat, and props design by Krista Montoya. The Production Stage Manager was Rachel Ducat. The Assistant Stage Manager was Harper Hadley. The Board Operator was Chyanne Huynh. The cast was as follows:

KATHLEEN ABEDON . . . . Karen Slack
JO HUNTER . . . . Jada Suzanne Dixon

CHARACTERS

KATHLEEN ABEDON – 40s. A grieving working-class mother of an alleged mass shooter. Kathleen is angry, contentious, and fighting boldly for her late son's legacy.

JOSEPHA (JO) HUNTER – Mid-30s. A journalist of some distinction, with one successful book to her name. Resourceful, driven, and manipulative, Jo's professional demeanor almost conceals her vulnerabilities.

SETTING

A modest apartment in Mecklenburg,
a small town in the eastern United States.

TIME

Late summer, present day.

AUTHOR'S NOTES

Truth Be Told is to be performed without an intermission. Approximate running time is ninety-five minutes.

ACKNOWLEDGEMENTS

The author would like to thank the following individuals and organizations for their kind support, help, and encouragement:

Jackie Apodaca

Nancy Bach

Karyn Morris Brownlee

T.S. Frank

Michelle Park

Francesca Ravera

Kim T. Sharp

Spencer Whale

Ashland New Plays Festival

Dayton Playhouse

The University of Puget Sound Theatre Department

Wagner College Theatre Department

To my mother Edwina,
my son Max,
and my wife Susan,
who did such a splendid job of raising our son.

Scene One

(*Present day. Late summer. Monday morning. A modest apartment, combination living/dining room with a sectioned-off kitchen.*)

(*It feels as if the tenant hasn't quite finished moving in. There are unpacked boxes stacked against the walls, each one of them written on with a Sharpie – "kitchen," "bedroom," "bath," etc. While the apartment is neat and clean, it's also cramped and claustrophobic.*)

(**JO**, *thirties, casual chic, is setting up her work area on a small coffee table, where a laptop computer already sits.*)

(**KATHLEEN**, *forties, her attire a less-than-successful attempt at sophistication, stands waiting nervously.*)

KATHLEEN. Would you like some coffee?

JO. Not just yet, Kathleen, thank you. Had two cups at breakfast. So...

KATHLEEN. You already told me that, didn't you?

(**JO** *smiles, goes back to work; she looks for space.*)

Do you need more room? I could move some of these boxes.

JO. No, I'm fine.

KATHLEEN. *(As she starts to pick up a box.)* I meant to make more space before you came but I –

JO. Kathleen, I have plenty of room.

(**KATHLEEN** *sets the box down.)*

KATHLEEN. I wish we coulda done this at the house.

JO. I thought you sold the house.

KATHLEEN. Yeah, needed the money. Wanted to get out of this crummy town.

JO. Yet you're still here. Mecklenburg. Why haven't you left?

KATHLEEN. Where am I gonna go? No family, no money –

JO. What about the money from the house?

KATHLEEN. I got maybe half of what the house was worth, and that's going fast. At least I got a job here in Mecklenburg. Sure, people look at me funny, but I still get a paycheck.

JO. I see.

(**JO** *nods, goes back to work, taking a small electronic device from her bag.)*

KATHLEEN. What's that?

JO. *(Handing it to* **KATHLEEN.***)* Oh, that's the voice recorder. Remember we talked about it.

KATHLEEN. Right, I remember… It's sticky.

JO. Sticky? Oh, maple syrup.

KATHLEEN. What?

JO. My five-year-old, Jake. He likes to play with the recorder.

(*She takes it from* **KATHLEEN**, *touches it, laughs.)*

Yesterday morning he insisted on recording himself eating breakfast. Waffles. We listened to it several times.

(**JO** *laughs,* **KATHLEEN** *smiles.*)

KATHLEEN. That's cute. Is Jake here in Mecklenburg with you?

JO. Oh, no. He's home with his daddy.

KATHLEEN. Is that hard? I mean, writing these books, don't you have to go away a lot?

JO. Quite a bit in the last year, that's for sure.

KATHLEEN. And Jake, he doesn't mind?

JO. I took him with me on my book tour last year. That was an adventure.

KATHLEEN. How so?

JO. Oh, it was my first book tour and I had no idea how hectic it would be. My agent tried to warn me but... I thought I was Supermom. So I sent him home. Jake missed his daddy. You should see the two of 'em. They're good buddies. It's sweet.

(**JO** *smiles, goes back to setting up her work area. Beat.*)

KATHLEEN. I liked your book. *Evil Men*...something. I liked it a lot.

JO. Oh, you read it. Thank you so much, Kathleen. Means a lot to me.

KATHLEEN. What's the book called again?

JO. *The Evil That Men Do.*

KATHLEEN. Right. Did you make that up?

JO. It's from Shakespeare. *Julius Caesar.* "The evil that men do lives after them / The good is oft interréd with their bones."

KATHLEEN. What's that mean?

JO. Well, in the play, after Julius Caesar is assassinated, Marc Antony does a speech, very famous, "Friends, Romans, countrymen, lend me your ears." You've heard that, I'm sure.

    (Short beat.)

Anyway, he argues that when someone dies, we tend to remember only the bad, the evil that a person does. The good is buried with him. Forgotten.

KATHLEEN. Forgotten. Right. That's what happens. And that's why I liked your book, 'cause I... I mean, Aynesworth, that man you wrote about, I forget his first name.

JO. Robert.

KATHLEEN. Robert Aynesworth. I know he did those terrible things – murdered his wife and his little girl and he took his little boy on that boat, that voyage and then...terrible but...when you read about him, Aynesworth, you feel sorry for him, kind of. Not sorry but...like, sympathize, 'cause you know he had some good in him...somewhere. That's what I want, when they read our book. I want people to feel something for my Julian. Not just hate and anger. I don't want the good to be forgotten. Because Julian deserves that, just like any other human being...

    (Brimming with emotion, her voice cracks.)

...he deserves that.

    *(**KATHLEEN** nods, a bit shaky. **JO** crosses to her.)*

JO. I know this can't be easy, my being here, stirring all this up again.

KATHLEEN. I just don't know if I can... I don't know.

JO. I understand.

> (**KATHLEEN** *sighs deeply, trying to regain composure.*)

Look, I'm a mother, too. That is no small bond between us, believe me. And had I been in your place, I –

KATHLEEN. You're not in my place.

JO. No. But I have a son. I cherish his future. I fear for his safety and comfort in a wicked world. You felt the same about Julian, I'm sure. A minute ago you said you wanted people to feel something for him, something besides hate and anger. I want that, too. That's the story I'd like to write. The mother's story.

> (**JO** *takes her hand.*)

So, tell me all about Julian, all about that boy you loved so much. Please.

> (**KATHLEEN** *sighs, then nods her assent.*)

Thank you. Now...where will you be sitting?

KATHLEEN. Wherever you want me.

JO. I want you where you'll be most comfortable.

> (**KATHLEEN** *crosses to a stuffed chair and taps it.*)

KATHLEEN. Here.

JO. Perfect.

> (**KATHLEEN** *sits,* **JO** *sitting opposite her.* **JO** *puts the recording device on the table in front of* **KATHLEEN**.)

KATHLEEN. Oh, um, how do I say your name?

JO. You mean...Jo?

KATHLEEN. I thought it was *Josepha*.

JO. I prefer Jo*sepha*. But just call me Jo. Everyone does. Ready?

> (**KATHLEEN** *nods.*)

Great. Now –

KATHLEEN. Oh, wait.

> (**KATHLEEN** *rises, crosses to a small desk, and pulls out a stack of five-by-seven index cards secured in a rubber band. She sits back in her chair.*)

Ready.

> (**KATHLEEN** *takes the rubber band off the cards and starts to lay them out on a coffee table in front of her. She holds onto two cards stapled together.* **JO** *watches this suspiciously for a moment, turns on the voice recorder, and speaks into it.*)

JO. My name is Josepha Hunter and I am here for my initial interview with Kathleen Abedon, mother of Julian Abedon. The date is September sixteenth. The time is 9:27 a.m. Now, I'd like to start with –

KATHLEEN. I want to start with this.

> (**KATHLEEN** *holds up the two index cards stapled together.*)

JO. With what?

> (**KATHLEEN** *pulls on a pair of glasses and reads from the cards.*)

KATHLEEN. On the morning of Friday, August tenth, last year, my seventeen-year-old son, Julian –

JO. Wait. I'm sorry, what are you reading, exactly?

KATHLEEN. I wrote this. I want to start with it, OK? Then you can ask me questions, but this really needs to be in the book.

JO. It needs to be in the book?

(**KATHLEEN** *removes her glasses, looks at* **JO**.)

You can read it, of course. I'm sorry if I –

KATHLEEN. *(Reads.)* On the morning of Friday, August –

JO. But I need to stress that what goes in the book is ultimately my decision. Mine alone. You understand that, right?

KATHLEEN. You'll want this in the book, I promise.

(She puts her glasses back on, reads.)

On the morning of Friday, August tenth, last year, my seventeen-year-old son, Julian Abedon, reported for his summer job at the Eden's Bounty food warehouse here in Mecklenburg. There was gunfire. Fourteen employees of the warehouse, including Julian, died and another was seriously injured. This was a terrible tragedy and I, like so many other parents before me, have now lost a child to an act of violence. My son Julian had a difficult upbringing. His father died less than a month after Julian was born and he was raised by me, his mother, and his stepfather, Harlan Kenney.

(Short beat.)

Harlan Kenney is also deceased. Even though I married Harlan, I kept the name of Abedon since it was also the name of my only child. Julian was pronounced guilty for the killings at the warehouse. There was no trial, although an investigation revealed many facts – such as from survivors who claim they saw Julian firing a weapon. But these are only claims and it seems unlike Julian to do that and I knew him like no one else.

KATHLEEN. The whole truth has yet to come out and I hope this book will correct that.

    (**KATHLEEN** *removes her glasses, puts the cards down.* **JO** *regards her, makes a few notes.* **JO** *reaches for Kathleen's notecard.*)

JO. May I see that?

    (**KATHLEEN** *hands her the card,* **JO** *scans it. After a beat, she reads aloud.*)

"Harlan Kenney is also deceased."

    (**JO** *looks to* **KATHLEEN***, who nods.*)

You don't mention how Harlan died.

KATHLEEN. The official story is that Julian, um, shot Harlan at home before leaving for the warehouse.

JO. The official story?

    (**KATHLEEN** *nods tersely.*)

I see.

    (**JO** *goes back to the card.*)

Nor do you mention that Harlan worked at the warehouse with Julian. He was his supervisor, correct?

KATHLEEN. Yeah, but Harlan wasn't there when the shootings happened.

JO. No, he was at home, dead. Julian had already shot him by –

KATHLEEN. We don't know that.

JO. We don't know what?

KATHLEEN. That Julian shot Harlan.

JO. I'm confused, um... Are you saying that –

KATHLEEN. I'm saying that there are no witnesses to Harlan's murder. I was still at work. Night shift. Nobody saw it except for two people who are now dead. What I do know is that what everyone said Julian did –

JO. You mean murdering his stepfather or –

KATHLEEN. I mean everything. All of it.

JO. All of it?

KATHLEEN. All of it! You didn't know Julian. I did and all those things that he... I mean, that they said he... It was very much unlike him –

JO. Just to be clear –

KATHLEEN. – very much unlike him and who knew Julian better than me? Nobody. That's what I'm saying.

JO. I see.

> *(Beat.)*

This is a departure.

KATHLEEN. What do you mean?

JO. From the time I originally approached you, through all of our correspondence...and perhaps I missed something, but it always seemed to me that you knew Julian was the shooter.

KATHLEEN. I never said that. I never even thought that, not completely.

JO. Oh.

> *(**JO** makes a note.)*

KATHLEEN. You seem disappointed.

JO. Disappointed? No, I just want to be clear. Are you saying that Julian didn't –

KATHLEEN. I'm saying that nobody knows everything about... I mean, who could, but... There are questions.

JO. I agree. There are plenty of unanswered questions.

KATHLEEN. You seem so disappointed.

JO. Don't be silly. I'm intrigued, really. Now –

KATHLEEN. You never see his face.

JO. His face?

KATHLEEN. In the movie, the video, you never see his face. The shooter. Security cameras were broken.

JO. One of two cameras in the workers' lounge was not working, true, but –

KATHLEEN. It says so in the report. You only see the shooter from the back.

JO. That's correct.

(*Short beat.*)

Have you seen the video?

KATHLEEN. No. Have you?

JO. Yes. And you're right, you never see the shooter's face. But we do see him from behind –

KATHLEEN. Just for a few seconds.

JO. Just for a few seconds, yes. But we clearly see him carrying the automatic rifle, the Remington Adaptive Combat rifle. On his waist, we see the Glock 19 –

KATHLEEN. (*A bit testy.*) I know.

JO. Sorry, Kathleen, I'm just trying to understand. When you say these are only claims, what exactly –

KATHLEEN. Since one of the cameras was broken, you never see the shooter's face. So, the movie doesn't prove that it was Julian. It doesn't.

JO. I see.

(She makes a note, puts her pen down, and looks hard at **KATHLEEN***.)*

Julian walks into the –

*(***KATHLEEN*** starts to protest.)*

The shooter…walks into the workers' lounge at 6:57 a.m. Shift change at seven, so it's crowded. Twenty-one people are present. The shooter opens fire. Fourteen die. One is seriously injured. Seven get away unharmed. Can we agree on that?

*(***KATHLEEN*** nods curtly.)*

All eight survivors identify Julian as the shooter. Now, eyewitness testimony can be notoriously unreliable, but in this case –

KATHLEEN. Right. And a lot of times, eyewitnesses, they like… Especially in a thing where there's lots of panic, they don't… I mean, you're scared. Who knows what you really saw? Right? Also, Julian, he was wearing those…

JO. Fatigues?

KATHLEEN. Fatigues, right. And he had on that hat. What do they call it?

JO. Field cap.

KATHLEEN. Right. So, Julian looked different – it's not like he went to work every day wearing fatigues and a field cap. Right? Plus, I saw him in that, um, field cap a couple of times. Once he had it down so far over his face, I almost didn't recognize him, so… See what I mean?

JO. So, you acknowledge that Julian was wearing the fatigues?

KATHLEEN. Yeah. I mean, the shooter was.

JO. And when the police found Julian's body, a short time later, he was dressed in those same fatigues. Is that correct?

(*Beat.* **KATHLEEN** *turns from* **JO**.)

Kathleen, may I tell you something? About myself?

(**KATHLEEN** *nods tentatively.*)

Some time ago, Jake, my little boy, he hit someone. Another, you know...little boy. I saw it happen, and it shocked me. How angry he got. How hard he swung his little fist. If someone had told me about it, I would've said, no, not my sweet little boy. No! But seeing it...that was different. And the guilt that I felt in that moment –

KATHLEEN. That's not what this is about –

JO. The guilt was so strong that, even though I'd seen it happen, my immediate impulse was to deny it. So, I understand how you could feel –

KATHLEEN. This is not about what I feel, it's about what I know! It's about the facts. There are facts in dispute.

JO. Fair enough, there are certainly facts in dispute. Tell you what, let's back up and –

KATHLEEN. Bob and Sally Dunbar, you know who they were?

JO. The Dunbars, from the warehouse, married couple.

KATHLEEN. Yeah. Julian liked them. They came to the house for cookouts a couple times and they were sweet with him, especially Sally, But still, they were killed. If he liked them, why would he kill them?

JO. I don't know.

KATHLEEN. And nobody saw Julian shoot Harlan. Report doesn't say that. Just says he did it, but nobody saw it.

(**JO** *starts to speak.*)

And we don't even know for sure that Julian shot himself. Nobody saw it. No video cameras, nothing.

JO. If I may, Kathleen, the bullet that killed Julian came from his gun. The Glock 19 that he used to shoot Har–

(**KATHLEEN** *starts to protest.*)

– that he allegedly used to shoot Harlan. That same gun was used on Julian and that gun was found –

KATHLEEN. On the floor. The gun was found on the floor a few feet from Julian, but CNN said it was in his hand. Wrong! Lots of news things... Reports that day were wrong, just wrong. Like, um... One of 'em, they said there were two, maybe three shooters and that some of the shots came from outside the warehouse, in the alley, and then a man –

JO. In the rush to get on the –

KATHLEEN. Let me finish! There was a man, an older man, he was in the alley during the shooting. And one of the news people, I forget who, he said that man from the alley was one of the shooters. He said so, right on the air.

JO. The man's name is Anthony Bova. He owns a carpentry studio across the alleyway. He heard the commotion and came running into the alley. And CNN eventually corrected the story by –

KATHLEEN. That's not my point!

(*Beat.*)

JO. I'm sorry, Kathleen. What is your point?

KATHLEEN. Just that there are questions. About the gun in Julian's hand and the security cameras and... I don't know, but you add that to everything else, with CNN and the security cameras and the...the field cap and that man in the alley and Bob and Sally Dunbar. There are just all these questions and... I'm not explaining it right. Alan could tell you better what –

JO. Alan? Who is Alan?

KATHLEEN. He's a... He called me. We've been...talking about what happened that day.

JO. You've been talking about what happened to...Alan. What does he want?

KATHLEEN. He doesn't want anything. He just –

JO. He wants something, Kathleen, trust me. God, I hope he's not a writer, because –

KATHLEEN. He's not a writer! And he doesn't want anything! Look, he's very nice. He just wanted to talk to me about that day. About my son.

> *(Takes a deep breath, then looks squarely at* **JO**.*)*

Alan said he wasn't convinced that Julian was guilty. See, and I'd been thinking all along that... Well, it just never seemed like Julian to... Especially that week 'cause he seemed good. Happy almost. But then the police report came out and all the news people, they said Julian did it, and so... But it always bothered me. And then Alan came here to see me, and I said all this to him and he believed me. And he told me stuff, too, like about CNN and stuff they said. And Alan said there was evidence, real evidence that Julian was... I forget what he called it...someone to blame.

JO. A scapegoat?

KATHLEEN. A scapegoat. Yes. And Alan's very smart. And he cares. I mean, he came all the way from Arizona just to –

JO. Arizona? Wait, I hope you don't mean Alan Covington.

KATHLEEN. Do you know him?

JO. Alan Covington came to see you? He flew up here, came to this apartment?

KATHLEEN. Yes.

JO. When?

KATHLEEN. Last Wednesday.

JO. Last Wednesday?! Five days ago?

      (**KATHLEEN** *nods.*)

And so, this is all coming from Alan Covington? This new-found skepticism about Julian's guilt, about –

KATHLEEN. It's not new-found. I just told you, I always thought there were things that... Like the Dunbars! But then Alan, he said a lot of stuff I never thought about and realized or... Do you know Alan? 'Cause it sounds like you –

JO. I know who he is. I'm curious, did you tell Alan Covington that I was interviewing you for a book?

KATHLEEN. No.

      (**JO** *opens a laptop computer, clicks away.*)

Look, Alan's a nice man. He... What are you doing?

JO. Do you have Wi-Fi in here?

KATHLEEN. I don't know, my computer died and I never got a new one, so –

JO. I'm not getting a signal.

KATHLEEN. Please tell me what you're doing.

JO. I'm trying to see if he's talked about you on his show or tweeted about you or –

KATHLEEN. I don't underst–

JO. Kathleen, you and I have an exclusive arrangement. That means you can speak to me and only me about the events of August tenth of last year, and about everything leading up to that date and since. You cannot speak to another writer or –

KATHLEEN. Alan's not a writer.

JO. He has a podcast, a website, he's all over Twitter, and if he has already mentioned you in any context then we have a problem. My lawyer, my god, she'll throw a –

KATHLEEN. He listened to me! He cared about me, Alan did. And he told me things I had never thought of before. Like the gun not being in Julian's hand. 'Cause on CNN they said –

JO. What CNN said on the day of the shooting, as it was happening, has no bearing on the facts of the case –

KATHLEEN. Why not?

JO. – and for Alan Covington to suggest that it does is irresponsible at best and –

KATHLEEN. You've already decided, haven't you? You think Julian did it and you won't even listen to –

JO. Kathleen –

KATHLEEN. You think Julian did it. As soon as I read my statement, you were all disappointed. It's like you don't even care about the truth, you just –

JO. I care deeply about the truth. And yes, I do have an opinion of what occurred on August tenth, but I am not here to impose my beliefs on you. But by involving Alan Covington, we –

KATHLEEN. Alan is a nice man. I don't understand why –

JO. He is not a nice man.

KATHLEEN. He was nice to me!

(Beat.)

JO. I'm sorry, Kathleen, I understand how Covington might have... Look, let me explain why exclusivity is so important in this –

KATHLEEN. Who cares?

JO. If you tell your story to Alan Covington and he slaps it all over his website where people can read it for free, then who's gonna buy our book? Understand?

(**KATHLEEN** *nods curtly.*)

I'm simply trying to protect my work. *Our* work!

KATHLEEN. This was a mistake. Never should have said yes to this.

JO. Kathleen –

KATHLEEN. I think you should leave.

JO. Leave?

KATHLEEN. I can't do this book.

JO. We have a contract.

KATHLEEN. Not anymore. I want you out of my home.

JO. You realize that if I leave, you'll have to return your advance.

KATHLEEN. What?

JO. And the remaining balance will be withheld. It'll make my publisher happy. They didn't want to pay you in the first place. My journalist friends, they all think I'm crazy for paying a source. But I respect you, Kathleen. I wanted it to be the mother's story, so I got you the money.

KATHLEEN. I need that money. I gotta get out of this town. Go somewhere else, change my name, disappear. But I can't do that unless I have that money.

JO. Then the best thing for you to do –

KATHLEEN. Maybe your publisher can send me another writer. Someone, you know...nicer.

JO. Yeah, I get that a lot. Sorry, it doesn't work that way. I put this project together. There's nobody waiting in the wings.

*(**KATHLEEN** walks away. Beat.)*

JO. Kathleen, I'm sorry. I handled this badly. David, my husband, he says I'm too contrary. It's my degree in rhetoric, he says.

(She tries a self-deprecating laugh.)

This Alan Covington thing. I've let it become personal and I'm sorry. I will talk to my lawyer tonight and we'll figure it out. But for now, let's just put it aside and start over. Kathleen, please look at me.

*(**KATHLEEN** does so.)*

Don't you want the world to know that your boy wasn't some common criminal? Don't you want people to know there was goodness in him?

KATHLEEN. Yes. But it has to be the truth.

JO. It will be. The whole truth – about Julian, about the love you had for that boy. We will bring all of that into the light, I promise you. May I please stay?

*(A pause as **KATHLEEN** gains her composure.)*

KATHLEEN. I need some coffee. Do you want some?

JO. Two sugars.

*(**KATHLEEN** rises, crosses to the kitchen. **JO** sighs deeply.)*

(Blackout.)

Scene Two

(Ninety minutes later. **KATHLEEN** *reads aloud from one of her index cards. Several index cards have been turned upside down and put in a separate "discard" pile.)*

*(***JO*** *sits across from her with a notebook.)*

KATHLEEN. The death of my husband, George Abedon, was a devastating impact on us as a family. Julian was only a month old when George, his father, died in a car crash on his way home from work. It was raining, and he was trying to pass a truck carrying cars – You know, those trucks with the cars, like…all the cars piled up on the back? Know what I mean?

*(***JO*** *nods.)*

It was raining, and he was trying to pass a truck carrying cars, but he lost control of his car and it flipped over and went down a hill and crashed. He was killed instantly, and I know that the last thing to flash through his mind was his beautiful baby boy, Julian, who we named for George's beloved mother, Julia. It was a terrible personal tragedy for me. I received a settlement of money from the insurance company but it was not enough to pay for everything and so I had to get a job but also take care of my baby. It was a hard time for me. George's family helped some but not much as it was only his mother and his brother, and they didn't like me much, so I had to –

JO. Why didn't they like you?

KATHLEEN. Um, I kind of wanted to finish this part about George and then maybe you could ask me ques–

JO. Why didn't they like you, Kathleen?

KATHLEEN. George was... He kind of had to marry me. You know, 'cause –

(**JO** *writes in her notepad.*)

I don't want that in the book. I mean it's not like he didn't love me, and we would have gotten married anyway even if... But his mother kinda blamed me, like I was the only one in the room, you know. Please don't put that in the book.

JO. So, you and George were only married a short time?

KATHLEEN. Five and a half months. But I loved George and he loved me and if he'd lived things would've been different. I mean, not that Harlan was...

JO. Not that Harlan was what?

KATHLEEN. Nothing, George and me, no matter what his mother thought about us, we were in love and if he hadn't died... That's all I'm saying.

JO. How long had you been seeing George before you discovered you were pregnant?

KATHLEEN. See, that's not the kind of stuff I want in the book.

JO. How old were you?

KATHLEEN. Twenty thr– ...um, four. Twenty-four.

(*Back to the notecard, reading.*)

George's family helped some but... I'll skip over here... Umm, I had to get a job. I went back to work at JCPenney's where I had worked but quit right before Julian was born.

(*As* **KATHLEEN** *flips to a new card,* **JO** *takes the opportunity to speak.*)

JO. Kathleen, let's... Could we just talk for a while?

KATHLEEN. I thought we were.

JO. We are. But…and all your preparation, very helpful. It's still our first day and look how much ground we've covered. But I also think it might be a good idea for us to just chat. I'd like to hear what you have to say off the cuff.

KATHLEEN. But I have it all written down.

JO. And that's very helpful, it is, but it's my job to coax out some thoughts and memories that perhaps you haven't explored on your own.

KATHLEEN. Like what?

JO. Like, you've got a new baby, you've just lost your husband, you go back to work. Who's helping you with Julian?

> (**KATHLEEN** *thinks for a moment, then reaches for an index card from her pile.* **JO** *pulls the pile away from her.)*

Just tell me.

KATHLEEN. Like I said… *(Waving the index card.)* …in here, George's family helped some. His mother, but she was old, sick a lot. Kaylee, his brother's wife, she was sweet. I liked Kaylee and she was good with the baby but then they moved away so…

JO. And it would be a few more years before Harlan –

KATHLEEN. Right.

JO. So, there was no one. Except your mother.

> (**KATHLEEN** *shifts uncomfortably.* **JO** *checks a note.)*

Your father, he –

KATHLEEN. Gone. He left when I was…don't even know. I was a baby.

JO. Have you had any contact with –

KATHLEEN. No.

JO. But your mother, she was still alive at the time, and she lived in the area, correct?

> (**KATHLEEN** *nods.*)

So, you must have depended on her quite a bit.

KATHLEEN. I don't know if I want this in the book. About my mother.

JO. Why not?

> (**KATHLEEN** *doesn't budge. Beat.*)

I suppose if someone was writing a book about me, I wouldn't want my mother in it either.

> (**JO** *laughs amiably.*)

KATHLEEN. How come?

JO. No, no, no. Big mistake to start me talking about my mother. Be here for a month. OK, refocus. Where were –

KATHLEEN. What was so horrible about her?

JO. My mother? Oh, she wasn't horr– ...isn't horrible. I...look, we really need to focus on –

KATHLEEN. Geez, you wanna hear all this stuff about me, why can't you just...

> (**KATHLEEN** *shrugs.* **JO** *drops her notebook onto the table.*)

JO. OK, couple months ago. May. David, my husband, teaches journalism at a small liberal arts college – you wouldn't know it, never heard of it myself until he got the job. Anyway, David's a wonderful teacher and he received an award. Outstanding faculty, very prestigious, big end-of-the-year banquet. We hire a babysitter but three hours before the banquet, she cancels. Can't find anyone, last ditch, call my mother. "Mother, can you watch Jake for the evening?" "Yes, but your father can't drive, he has an infected foot." "Why can't you drive, Mother?" "Oh, I could never drive that far." Twenty minutes. So, fine, I hire an Uber, it brings her to the house. And didn't I tell you not to start me talking about my mother?

(She laughs. **KATHLEEN** *smiles politely.)*

Anyway, she calls my cell a few times during the banquet. I probably should've answered but it's David's night, so I turn off my phone, listen in peace to David's brilliant and charming speech. When I turn my phone back on twenty minutes later, there are four increasingly hysterical messages from my mother. "Come home, come home, come home!" I call her back, she doesn't answer. Now, I'm starting to panic so I drag David away from his adoring colleagues and students, get home and...

*(***JO*** *laughs, sips her coffee.)*

KATHLEEN. What was wrong?

JO. Jake wouldn't eat his lima beans. He refused to eat his lima beans because, let's face it, lima beans are awful. We wouldn't even have them in the house if my mother didn't buy them for us. Anyway, to my mother, not eating your lima beans is a major crisis, worthy of frantic phone calls and a spanking. To be fair, he did throw lima beans at her, but still, she spanked him, which we never do –

KATHLEEN. You've never spanked him?

JO. No.

KATHLEEN. Why not?

JO. I don't believe in spanking as a form of punishment for a small, defenseless child.

KATHLEEN. You didn't spank him after he hit that little boy?

JO. I've never spanked him.

KATHLEEN. Even on your book tour when he was getting on your nerves and –

JO. I never said he got on my nerves –

KATHLEEN. You sent him home.

JO. He missed his daddy. And I simply couldn't do my job with… Look, this is irrelevant to the –

KATHLEEN. So, there was never a time when you got angry or annoyed with him –

JO. Kathleen, please –

KATHLEEN. And just smacked him on the bottom or –

JO. No.

KATHLEEN. – swatted his face or grabbed him and –

JO. No!

> *(Short beat.)*

I'm sorry, Kathleen. I didn't mean to… I'm sorry.

> *(Tense beat. The two **WOMEN** look at each other for a moment.)*

OK. So, your mother –

KATHLEEN. I'm just gonna go back to reading –

JO. No.

> *(**JO** snatches the card from her.)*

I want to hear about your mother.

*(**KATHLEEN** gives her an icy stare.)*

She never married again. Talk about that.

*(Beat. **JO** waits her out.)*

Was she not interested? Did she date other men?

(Pause.)

KATHLEEN. She wanted to get married again. Didn't 'cause of me.

JO. Because of you. What do you mean?

KATHLEEN. She always said if she hadn't had me, she coulda...you know...

JO. No, I don't know.

KATHLEEN. "I'm still a good-looking woman." That's what Mom'd say. Every day, seemed like. "I'm still a good-looking woman. I'm still vital." I hate that word. Vital. "Some man'd be lucky to get his hands on a vital woman like me, let me tell you. And it woulda happened by now, wasn't for you. Wasn't for me havin' to drag you everywhere I go, havin' to spend all my money on hair curlers." 'Cept I don't remember her even trying to meet or go out with men or... Well, this one man. For a while. Didn't last. Who could blame him? Jesus, she was...

(Short beat.)

I shouldn't be talking like this. It's terrible to speak ill of the dead.

JO. It's not terrible, Kathleen. Not if it's the truth.

KATHLEEN. It is the truth. I wouldn't make something like that up.

JO. Of course not, I didn't mean to suggest –

KATHLEEN. If you're not gonna believe anything I –

JO. I believe you. I was simply –

KATHLEEN. Boy.

> *(Beat. **JO** sets down her notebook, looks at **KATHLEEN**.)*

JO. Kathleen, I'm very sorry that I snapped at you a moment ago. It was unprofessional and uncalled for. Can we agree that it's been a tense morning? Look... maybe we should take a short break and –

KATHLEEN. The whole world thinks I'm a monster.

JO. Oh, Kathleen, I don't believe –

KATHLEEN. I know what people think. Everywhere I go, "There she is. The mother." Every time I leave the apartment – which I never do unless I absolutely have to. Never go anywhere in this miserable town. People just...

JO. They what?

KATHLEEN. They think I'm a monster!

> *(She chokes back a tear.)*

The only person who's been even a little bit nice to me in all this time is Alan Covington. He's the only person who's treated me anything like a human being. Like a friend.

JO. I would like to be your friend, Kath–

KATHLEEN. Don't say that. You just want me to tell you stuff so you can write your book and...and if you write that I hated my mother on top of everything else, then people are just –

JO. Did you hate her?

KATHLEEN. Stop it! I was good to her. At the end, when she was sick and dying and mean and nasty as she could be, which was pretty goddamn nasty, I was there every day. Every day! Feeding her, washing her, wiping her...ugh. But for me or Julian, was she ever – no! Jesus, this one time...

(Short beat.)

JO. This one time, what?

*(**KATHLEEN** avoids her gaze.)*

This one time, what, Kathleen?

KATHLEEN. I don't want the whole world thinking I hated my mother!

JO. Fine, then we won't use it in the book. But tell me.

KATHLEEN. If you're not gonna use it, why should –

JO. Because I think you want to tell me.

(Beat.)

KATHLEEN. OK, this one day after working at Penney's, I stop at my mother's to pick up Julian but when I get to the house, nobody's there except for my little boy. As I find out later, my mother goes out to pick up her mail, falls down the front steps, breaks her ankle. Neighbors see her fall, call an ambulance, off to the hospital, but nobody – nobody – bothers to check inside the house where Julian was left alone for over four hours and he was only three years old. That woman just left him there. She didn't even think to call me at work or...or tell the people who came to help her, "My grandson's in the house." Something terrible could have happened. Somebody could've come in and... Or he could've gotten scared and run out or fallen or hurt himself or... But, no, when I got there Julian was sitting sweetly and quietly with *Goodnight Moon*, his favorite book. He couldn't read yet, but I had read it to him so many times that he knew it by heart. "Hush Mommy, hush." He kept saying that over and over. "Hush, Mommy, hush. The lady whispering hush." And he wasn't scared, he hadn't gotten hurt or soiled himself or made a mess in her precious rattrap of a house. He was very brave. And I picked him up and he hugged me so hard, squeezed me so tight and I never took him back in that house again, ever!

> *(Beat.)*

Hush, Mommy, hush. Over and over. Hushhh. That was my little boy. That was my Julian.

> *(**KATHLEEN** is shaking with emotion. Pause.)*

JO. Thank you, Kathleen.

> *(**KATHLEEN** looks at her, surprised by **JO**'s genuine response.)*

That story doesn't tell me you hated your mother. It tells me you loved your son.

> *(**JO** hands **KATHLEEN** a tissue. She takes it and wipes her eyes.)*

May I use it in the book?

> *(**KATHLEEN** shrugs. **JO** smiles.)*

I'll take that as a maybe.

> *(She makes a notation in her notebook.)*

Tell me another story.

KATHLEEN. About my mother?

JO. About your son.

> *(**KATHLEEN** smiles at her, starts going through her index cards.)*

> *(Blackout.)*

Scene Three

(The following day, Tuesday, late morning. Both **WOMEN** *dressed more casually.)*

*(***KATHLEEN*** animatedly moves around the room as she tells her story. She carries an index card but, at present, is not reading from it.)*

*(***JO*** sits listening, taking notes.)*

KATHLEEN. End of the school year, third grade – they had this, um…Spring Fling, they called it, so cute, and at each desk in the classroom, whoever sat at that desk had all their class projects and papers and drawings. But nobody's desk had as much…or as good, you know…as smart as Julian. All of his papers had A's on them and little stars and, um, you know, "Excellent" and "Very Good" and everything like that. His third grade teacher, Mrs. Hoover, she loved Julian. That night, she told me what a good boy he'd been all year. Delightful little boy, she called him. Delightful.

(She sighs contentedly.)

That was a good year, that third grade year.

JO. And Julian was how old?

KATHLEEN. He turned, um, nine in third grade.

*(***JO*** makes a note, then flips back in her book a few pages.)*

Right. February seventeenth. Ooh, that reminds me – that year, on his birthday, it was a Friday, I almost forgot this, and on Fridays Mrs. Hoover always had a special –

JO. Forgive me, Kathleen, but Julian's nine? When does his stepfather enter the picture? Earlier than nine, I thought.

(She goes to her computer.)

JO. Let's see. Yes, you're three years into your marriage to Harlan Kenney by this time, correct?

KATHLEEN. I guess so.

JO. Hm. OK, let's back up a little and –

KATHLEEN. What I wanted to tell you, see, Mrs. Hoover, she –

JO. We'll get there, I promise. Before we move too far ahead, though, I think it's important we go back and fill in some gaps in the timeline –

KATHLEEN. *(Urgently, getting* **JO***'s full attention.)* But every Friday, Mrs. Hoover, she'd have this special thing. Student of the week and on that day, Julian was named student of the week. On his birthday!

(She picks up her index cards and searches.)

I must have written a card about it.

JO. Thank you. But right now, I think we need to move on to some other factors in Julian's life.

KATHLEEN. Like what?

JO. Harlan Kenney, Julian's stepfather. Can you tell me –

*(***KATHLEEN*** flips through her index cards, finds one, and holding it up.)*

KATHLEEN. OK, we will, but one more story about –

JO. No, I want to hear about Har–

KATHLEEN. You're gonna love this. This happened that summer right after –

JO. No, I'd really like to move on.

KATHLEEN. Oh.

JO. Sorry, Kathleen, I'm just worried about time. It's Tuesday, I'm only scheduled here through tomorrow and there is so much other ground to cover. So, let's move on. Please?

> (**KATHLEEN** *nods.*)

Good. Harlan Kenney, tell me how the two of you met.

KATHLEEN. Don't you know this already? From your research.

JO. *(Checking her computer.)* No. I have the date of your wedding – October nine. But I don't know how you and Harlan met.

> (*Beat.* **KATHLEEN** *reluctantly puts her index card down.*)

KATHLEEN. Girl at work, Macie. She knew him from… around. Set us up. Thought we'd like each other.

JO. And did you?

KATHLEEN. Mm-hm.

JO. What was it about Harlan that drew you to him?

KATHLEEN. Um… He had a pretty good job with, um, benefits. I mean, he was nice to me and… You know, he bought me stuff. Dinner, flowers a few times. Shoes. We were out one night, and I walked past a shoe store and saw a pair of shoes I liked, and he said, "I'll buy 'em for you." And he did. I still have them.

> (*Beat.* **JO** *waits for more.*)

I needed to find somebody 'cause…I needed help and Harlan, he…

JO. He what?

KATHLEEN. He could be really sweet, Harlan could. And so I thought, maybe he could be a daddy for Julian. And that's what I wanted more than anything. For Julian to have a daddy, you know, like other kids. And so when Harlan said, "Let's get married," I said OK.

JO. So, did Julian get along with his new daddy?

KATHLEEN. Mm-hm.

(*Beat.*)

I mean, at first... Julian, he was only five, never had a man in his life, so...

JO. I see. Did Harlan make an effort to –

KATHLEEN. Of course, he did. He bought him stuff. Harlan played hockey when he was a kid, thought maybe Julian'd like it, so he bought him a stick and some roller blades. No, didn't like that. Harlan took him to a baseball game. No, didn't like that. Football, no didn't like that. And I said, "Look, Julian, look what your daddy brought you" and "Whyn't you go outside and play catch with Daddy" ...But Julian, he was never that kinda boy. Sports and... But Harlan, he did try.

JO. Were there signs of trouble between Harlan and Julian early on?

KATHLEEN. What do you mean by trouble?

JO. Let me rephrase the –

KATHLEEN. No, just say what you mean.

(*Beat.*)

JO. When did the abuse begin?

KATHLEEN. I hate that word. Abuse. It's a fuzzword.

JO. A what?

KATHLEEN. A fuzzword, that's what Alan calls it. I know you don't like him but even you gotta admit he has a point.

JO. About what?

KATHLEEN. Fuzzwords! Like abuse. That's a fuzzword because you say it and it just gets people stirred up, you know, emotionally.

JO. That's a fair point.

KATHLEEN. And what does it even mean, you know? Jesus, the TV people, they love to throw that word around but you can tell they don't even know what it means.

JO. We're not on TV right now, Kathleen. And between the two of us, I think we know what abuse means.

(**KATHLEEN** *huffs and looks away. After a beat,* **JO** *pulls a document from her file.*)

OK, let's switch gears. Yesterday you told me that in first grade, Julian got into a lot of fights.

(**KATHLEEN** *nods.*)

In second grade that seems to have escalated.

KATHLEEN. I never said that.

JO. I'm going by his school records.

(*Reads from the document.*) Violent tendencies. Difficulty making friends. Angry little boy –

KATHLEEN. But by third grade, he had gotten better. At Spring Fling, Julian's desk had more things than any other kid.

JO. And where was Harlan during that third grade year? There were periods of separation, correct?

(*She pulls a sheet of paper from a file folder.*)

I found an address change for Harlan and I assume –

KATHLEEN. Yes, there were periods of separation. What are you asking me?

JO. Was Harlan living with you during Julian's third grade year?

KATHLEEN. I think so. Part of it, anyway. I don't really remember.

> *(Beat. **JO** waits her out.)*

I think he left... Well, yeah, he did, he left. There was a big blow-up at Thanksgiving, at his mother's and we... I can't remember but Harlan...

> *(**KATHLEEN** makes a vague gesture suggesting that he "went away.")*

JO. What was the blow-up about?

KATHLEEN. What difference does it make if Harlan was living with us or not? It was a really good year. Why can't the book just say that?

JO. There is compelling evidence that your son and your husband had a volatile relationship and we –

KATHLEEN. Like what?

JO. Well...Harlan's murder for one thing.

KATHLEEN. Nobody saw Julian kill Harlan.

JO. True. But if we look at the nature of the crime –

KATHLEEN. The nature?

JO. It was brutal.

KATHLEEN. Well, yeah, it was a murder.

JO. Fifteen shots. Julian walked in –

KATHLEEN. Nobody saw Julian pull –

JO. The assailant walked into the bathroom where Harlan was showering and emptied an entire clip into his body, two shots directly into his head.

KATHLEEN. Yeah, I remember.

JO. It was personal. And you're right, nobody saw Julian do it, but if it was Julian, it tells us something about the nature of his relationship with –

KATHLEEN. It wasn't Julian.

> (**JO** *starts to speak.*)

It wasn't Julian!

> (*Short beat.*)

JO. There is also the testimony of Emily Murdock.

KATHLEEN. Gimme a break. Emily Murdock. That woman, she makes all these claims about Harlan at the warehouse and how he did this to Julian and that to Julian. But she's just pissed off at the world, 'cause…I mean, who could believe her? She'd say anything after –

> (*She stops herself suddenly, looks away.*)

JO. After what? Being shot in the back and paralyzed from the waist down? Yeah, that'd piss me off, too.

KATHLEEN. What I'm saying is… OK, Harlan kicked Julian. That was her whole thing, right?

JO. There was the kicking incident, yes, but Emily also spoke of verbal abuse, in front of Julian's co-workers –

KATHLEEN. Oh, please.

JO. – of Harlan hitting Julian more than once. There was –

KATHLEEN. Yeah, but that's just the Murdock woman saying that. Why's she so perfect all of a sudden? And then, Jesus, those TV people, they get a hold of it and "Oh, the stepfather kicked the boy and that's why" blah blah, like that's some kinda proof –

JO. You don't think Harlan kicking your son is a –

KATHLEEN. He kicked him in the butt to get him going. Come on, he was seventeen, lazy. You know how kids are, and if you don't, you're gonna learn. So Harlan… What, you never saw anybody just…

(She kicks her leg to demonstrate.)

KATHLEEN. You know, "Get going," that kinda thing. Harlan did that around the house all the time so what's the –

*(**JO** makes a note in her notebook.)*

That is not abuse. But this Murdock woman, she tells the cops and next thing you know the TV people are telling the whole world! "Troubled Boy's Violent History Revealed." That's what it said on the bottom of the screen. "Troubled Boy's Violent History Revealed" and I thought – no, I screamed at the TV, "That's my boy you're talking about! You don't know him, goddammit!" Shut it off, got rid of the damn thing. Good riddance.

JO. But were they wrong in saying that Julian had a violent history? There's plenty to indicate –

KATHLEEN. Stop it!

> *(**KATHLEEN** angrily picks up her coffee cup and exits into the kitchen.)*

> *(**JO** takes a deep sigh, sets her notebook down. She turns toward the kitchen, about to speak, when she sees a framed photo on a nearby desk. She crosses to it, picks it up, studies it.)*

> *(After a silence, **KATHLEEN** reenters, stirring her full coffee cup.)*

JO. Is this George? With you and the baby. Julian, I presume.

> *(**KATHLEEN** nods.)*

George was a nice-looking man. Do you have a favorite photo of Julian I could see?

*(**KATHLEEN** hesitates briefly but then puts her cup down and crosses to the same desk, opens a drawer, and pulls out a framed photo. She hands it to **JO**, who studies it.)*

I can see you in Julian. The eyes.

KATHLEEN. I see his daddy.

JO. Mm-hm. The chin.

KATHLEEN. The smile.

JO. The smile, you're right.

*(Beat. **KATHLEEN** crosses to **JO**, takes the first photo from her, looks at it.)*

KATHLEEN. George used to rub his eyes this certain way. With the heel of each hand.

(She demonstrates.)

Like this. Julian did that. Exact same way. Always reminded me.

*(**KATHLEEN** looks at the picture.)*

JO. Jake likes to mow the lawn. He has his own little toy mower and every time David cuts the grass, Jake's right behind him. "I help you, Daddy." They come in afterwards, down some Gatorade. David wipes his mouth with the back of his hand...

(She demonstrates.)

And then Jake wipes his mouth with the back of his hand.

(She demonstrates.)

Exact same way.

*(**KATHLEEN** smiles at her. Beat.)*

JO. Kathleen –

KATHLEEN. Who does Jake look like? You or David?

JO. Well, let's see.

> (*JO retrieves a cell phone from her pocket, scrolls, holds it up for* **KATHLEEN** *to see.*)

KATHLEEN. He's got your eyes.

JO. And his father's attitude.

> (*JO scrolls to another picture on her phone.*)

And there's his daddy.

> (*Scrolls again.*)

The three of us.

> (**KATHLEEN** *looks hard at the photo for a moment; she looks over to the framed photo in her hand, then back to the phone.*)

KATHLEEN. So, why'd he do it?

JO. Do what?

KATHLEEN. Why'd Jake punch the other little kid?

JO. Oh.

> (*JO pockets her phone, crosses away.*)

He just... It was silly, really. The little girl, she was... I don't know if I can explain it.

KATHLEEN. Little girl? You said it was a little boy.

> (*Short beat.*)

He hit a little girl?

JO. Yes. I was ashamed that he did it at all and the fact that it was a little girl, somehow made it... I don't know.

KATHLEEN. Troubled boy's violent history revealed.

> (**KATHLEEN** *gives* **JO** *a hard stare before taking the photos back to the desk.* **JO** *watches her carefully.)*

JO. Kathleen, I'm sorry that I –

KATHLEEN. Lied to me?

JO. Yes.

> *(Beat.)*

Look, why don't we order ourselves a nice lunch? Something rich and fattening and –

KATHLEEN. So why'd he hit the little girl?

JO. Kathleen –

KATHLEEN. Don't worry. We won't use it in the book.

> *(Beat.)*

JO. I took Jake to this class, Playful Parenting. "Joining children in their world of play." Anyway, we played this game called "robot" and one child is the robot and the other is the commander and the commander tells the robot what to do and where to go and then they switch, and the commander becomes the robot. But Jake would not switch. He would not be the robot. "No!" And I said, "Jake, honey, it'll be fun. Look, look at me," and I walked like the robot and he said, "No! No! Commander, commander!" and the little girl, his partner, she was, "My turn to be commander," and he said, "No!" and she said, "My turn now," and he...hit her. Not just a harmless swat, no, he punched her in the face. Hard. Would've hit her a second time if I hadn't grabbed his hand away. Her little nose, blood started pouring out like somebody turned on a faucet, all over her perfect little pink outfit. Looked like this pint-sized Jackie Kennedy. She screams – "ahhh" and the mother – "Look what your little monster did to my baby!"

KATHLEEN. You didn't spank him then?

JO. No, we do not... I grabbed him. He just kept saying, "No. Commander, commander!" And I... Before I even knew what I was doing, I grabbed him. "Why did you do that?" And I shook him.

> *(Clenching her fists, shaking "Jake" hard.)*

"Why did you do that?!"

> *(She stops shaking.)*

I was so ashamed. I immediately reached for him again, to hold him, to hug him. "Jake, honey, I'm sorry," but he pulled away. He...

> *(She folds her arms across her chest to demonstrate Jake's reaction.)*

And he had...

> *(She pats her biceps.)*

...these red marks from where I... And by the time David got home that night, there were bruises. David asked me what happened, and I couldn't even... Jake finally said, "Mommy got mad."

> *(Beat.)*

Jake is the love of my life. But truth be told, ever since...

> *(**JO** shakes her head, her voice trailing off.)*

KATHLEEN. Ever since what?

JO. Nothing.

KATHLEEN. So, what, now you're afraid your little boy's gonna shoot up a warehouse when he's –

JO. No, I am not afraid of that.

KATHLEEN. You sure? He's already smacking little girls around and throwing lima beans at his grandma. Sounds to me like –

JO. That's enough.

KATHLEEN. Now you know how I feel. Being accused of... people asking all these... Now you know how I feel.

JO. I want to know how you feel, Kathleen. That's my job, that's why I'm here. When I ask about Julian or Harlan, anything, I am not judging you.

> (**KATHLEEN** *quietly emits a scornful laugh.*)

I am in no position to judge anybody, I know that. But it's my job to ask these questions. If I don't ask the difficult questions, we're never going to get at the truth. And that's what I want. It's what we both want, isn't it?

KATHLEEN. Yes.

JO. Good.

> *(She sighs.)*

Oh, good. Thank you, Kathleen, that makes me feel –

KATHLEEN. That's why you need to talk to Alan Covington.

JO. What?

KATHLEEN. He gave me his number. He can tell you what he told me about Julian and the shooting and all the stuff the TV people got wrong. I can't remember everything and I'm no good at explaining so...

> *(Finding what she was looking for, she holds up a business card.)*

Here. Here's his number.

JO. No.

KATHLEEN. You said you want the truth. This is the truth.

JO. You and I still have a lot of work to do and –

KATHLEEN. Why won't you talk to him?

JO. Right now, I'm worried about efficiently using our time together or –

KATHLEEN. Why won't you talk to Alan?

(Beat.)

JO. Do you remember the killings at the newspaper in Virginia, February?

KATHLEEN. I don't watch the news anymore.

JO. Richmond suburb, man carries an AR-15 into a newspaper office. Six people dead. Alan Covington goes on the radio and declares that the six journalists who died – never mind that one of them was a receptionist and another was a teenage intern – the six journalists "had it coming." They all had it coming because they were journalists and, well, we all know about journalists. Covington gets a little backlash, then all of a sudden, his story changes. Now, he says, the shootings never happened at all. Nobody died. They were crisis actors! The whole thing was fake, staged by some liberal anti-gun –

KATHLEEN. Maybe it was. How do you know?

JO. I know because one of the men killed was my friend. David's closest friend, the best man at our wedding. Shot in the face six times. Jesus, they couldn't even have an open casket, because...

(She chokes back a tear.)

His poor wife, his sweet little girl, I've never seen such heartbreak. And I'm pretty sure they weren't play-acting just to piss off the NRA!

(Beat.)

KATHLEEN. I'm sorry about your friend, but…

JO. But what?

KATHLEEN. I don't know, sounds like Alan got some bad information and just… It's not like he killed those people himself. He –

JO. You want to know why Alan Covington really came to see you?

KATHLEEN. I know why he really came to see me. He thinks Julian was falsely accused and –

JO. Day before he came to see you, he was in Big Stone Gap, Virginia, at the Wallens Ridge State Prison. He spent the day with James Arthur Roland.

KATHLEEN. I don't know who that –

JO. Roland is the man who murdered my friend in Virginia. Roland claims he didn't… Well, now he claims he didn't do it, since Covington got involved. Pleaded guilty but now says he was framed by the federal government.

KATHLEEN. What's that have to do with –

JO. Weekend before that, Covington was in Saint Peters, Missouri, with the parents of Nicholas Frank, teenager who murdered nine classmates during choir practice at his junior high school before shooting himself. Thanks to Covington, the parents are now convinced their son was recruited by an ultra-left faction of the –

KATHLEEN. How do you know all this? You can't –

JO. My lawyer made a few phone calls. And you, Kathleen, you were the third person Covington came to see in four days, all for the same purpose. The Justice Project, that's what he's working on, although I think it needs a snappier title. His basic theory is that this rash of mass shootings – Richmond, Saint Peters, Mecklenburg, anywhere, U.S.A. – it's all engineered by liberal extremists intent on overturning the second amendment.

KATHLEEN. I don't believe you!

JO. And here's how twisted this all is. Alan Covington doesn't even believe it himself. He just wants to piss off the NRA crowd, get them to listen to his podcast, go to his website, buy his custom camouflage outfits. It's all about money. And now you're part of it, Kathleen. Congratulations!

> *(Beat.)*

I am on your side, Kathleen, but I refuse to be associated with Alan Covington in any way. He's an opportunist and he –

KATHLEEN. What do you mean?

JO. I mean that he's taking selfish advantage of your situation without –

KATHLEEN. Then what are you?

JO. – concern for the truth or what is right or wrong or who he hurts or –

KATHLEEN. Then what are you? Aren't you taking advantage of my situation by –

JO. Kathleen –

KATHLEEN. You're gonna make money offa me, aren't you? So, who's the one taking selfish advant–

JO. I'm also the one who arranged for you to receive a sizable cash advance. Has Alan Covington offered you money?

> **(KATHLEEN** *huffs, looks away.)*

I didn't think so. And if you want to keep the money, do not speak to that man again.

(Beat.)

Maybe we can't be friends, but I do have your best interests at heart, Kath–

KATHLEEN. Thank you so much, Jo. So glad to have you protecting me from opportunists.

*(**JO** starts to speak.)*

I won't talk to Alan again.

*(**KATHLEEN** crosses to **JO**.)*

But you need to know something. Alan Covington, he believed me.

JO. Kathleen, I –

*(**JO** reaches for **KATHLEEN**'s hand, but she yanks it away, moves quickly to her chair and sits.)*

KATHLEEN. Let's just get this damn interview over with.

*(**JO** picks up her notebook and pen, faces **KATHLEEN**.)*

JO. OK. Tell me about Thanksgiving. Third grade.

*(They look at each other for a long beat. **KATHLEEN** sighs, readies herself.)*

KATHLEEN. Julian got sick. At the table.

JO. You mean he...threw up at the dinner table?

KATHLEEN. Yes.

(Short beat.)

Harlan's mother, Margaret... We were supposed to eat at two or three in the afternoon, but she took forever, and we ended up eating at five or...later and Julian was so hungry. All he'd had was a bowl of Froot Loops for breakfast, but Harlan didn't want him to spoil his appetite, so he wouldn't let him have anything else before dinner. So, when Margaret finally served the turkey, Julian ate really fast and I guess he ate too much. Two helpings of cranberry sauce, then dessert. Margaret made this really good pecan pie, sweet and sticky and Julian loved it, said he wanted a second piece and Margaret, she was, "Oh, please, as much as you like, sweetheart. Grandma knows you love it." And she cuts this big piece, piles on all this whipped cream. And I tried to tell Julian to slow down but Margaret, she just... "Oh, he's enjoying himself. Stop nagging him" and so I stopped but then he ate too much too fast and he got sick. It went everywhere. He was only eight, he didn't know better. Margaret, she's the one who should've been punished, the way she –

JO. Punished?

KATHLEEN.   Harlan was angry. OK? Julian had, you know... He did eat too fast and I think Harlan might've even said for him to slow down and...don't have more pie. And that was just the kinda thing that could make Harlan get so... Anyway, he made Julian...clean it up.

JO. The vomit?

KATHLEEN. Yes.

JO. Did you or Margaret help him to –

KATHLEEN. No. Harlan told us to leave the room. OK, here's why it wasn't abuse. It wasn't abuse because I didn't let it become abuse. I stopped it.

JO. How?

KATHLEEN. Like I said, Harlan told me to leave but I stayed right outside the door, so I could hear and... Harlan spanked him a few times and he kept saying "clean it up, clean it up" and Julian was crying which always made Harlan angry and Julian could usually stop but not this time, so then I heard Harlan say, "OK, if you're so hungry"...

(Choking back a tear.)

Harlan wasn't bad at heart, but he could get so –

JO. If you're so hungry, what?

KATHLEEN. If you're so hungry...eat this.

*(**JO** reacts audibly.)*

And I knew what he meant, and I tried to open the door, but it was locked and so I ran around to the kitchen and came in that way and I stopped it. Harlan, he was pushing Julian's face down in the...the mess on the table and Julian, he was crying, and I said, I screamed, "STOP IT! STOP IT NOW!!!" And I pushed him, Harlan, I pushed him as hard as I could, and he fell back and hit his head on a chair and then I grabbed Julian and pushed him through the kitchen door. And that was it.

JO. Was Harlan hurt?

KATHLEEN. No. Just stopped him long enough for Julian to get out.

JO. Did Harlan retaliate in any way?

KATHLEEN. What do you mean?

JO. Did he try and punish Julian further? Did he punish you?

KATHLEEN. No. He left.

JO. He left?

KATHLEEN. That night, after we got home. I told Harlan to leave.

JO. You threw him out?

KATHLEEN. Yes. I took care of my boy. Just like after I found him all alone in my mother's house, I never took him back there again. I took care of my boy. Put that in the book.

JO. I will.

> (**JO** *makes a note.*)

So, after Thanksgiving, Harlan moved out.

> (**KATHLEEN** *nods.*)

For how long?

KATHLEEN. That next summer. July, I guess. Harlan found the job at... He found a different job and wanted us to move there with him.

JO. And this was the supervisor job at the Eden's Bounty warehouse in Mecklenburg?

> (**KATHLEEN** *nods.*)

Did you consider not following him to Mecklenburg? After the Thanksgiving episode, did you ever consider leaving Harlan?

KATHLEEN. Harlan, he...he knew how upset I was about Thanksgiving and he was very sorry. He came to see me that spring and you could tell, he was... He just seemed so alone. But still, I told Harlan, "If we come back, Julian comes first."

JO. *(Writing it down.)* Julian comes first.

> (**KATHLEEN** *nods.*)

And what did Harlan say to that?

KATHLEEN. Oh, he agreed.

> (*Beat.* **JO** *waits her out.*)

A boy needs a father. I didn't have a father. I barely had a mother, so I know first-hand what it's like not to have any… And I wanted Julian to have what I never… What's so horrible about that?

JO. Nothing.

KATHLEEN. And it was a much better job that Harlan got, and for a lot more money. Not like that should be the only… Or even the most important… But that matters, too. And he was a good provider, whatever anybody says about him, Harlan was a good provider. Plus, it was a new town. Here in Mecklenburg… Which I thought'd be nicer… But still, it was a fresh start.

(**JO** *makes a note.*)

And so, we got here to Mecklenburg and we came to the new house – he bought us a new house. Bigger, with a yard, and a big kitchen and a nicer…everything. It was all just so much better than before. It just felt like…like a life. You know?

JO. Yes.

(*Beat.*)

So, things were better?

(**KATHLEEN** *offers a wan smile, but then looks away.* **JO** *waits* **KATHLEEN** *out for a long beat before pulling out a piece of paper, reading from it.*)

Fifth grade – suspended two days for fighting.

(**KATHLEEN** *offers no response.*)

Sixth grade – suspended three days for fight–

KATHLEEN. That boy attacked Julian. He was defending himself.

JO. Tell me about it.

KATHLEEN. Kid jumped on Julian, Julian punched him.

JO. It was in gym class, wasn't it?

KATHLEEN. The boy attacked him. Julian fought back. Julian got thrown out of school. End of story.

JO. I see.

> *(She makes a quick note, refers to another sheet of paper.)*

Also, in the sixth grade. Just before the holidays.

> *(**KATHLEEN** sighs, agitated.)*

Julian is suspended again, this time for...

> *(**JO** takes a closer look at the paper.)*

No, I take it back, he was expelled.

KATHLEEN. He wasn't expelled.

JO. The school record says he was expelled.

KATHLEEN. OK, yeah, he was, but they never actually... OK, the school had this hearing, said Julian'd be expelled unless he went through this program, therapy or whatever. What a joke. All they do is keep him out of school for a week and then I take him to some psychiatrist. Lady talks to him for like twenty minutes, "Don't do it again," blah blah. Back in school.

JO. But he pulled a knife on this little girl.

KATHLEEN. It was a box cutter.

JO. A box cutter?

KATHLEEN. From the warehouse. Harlan was always leaving 'em in his pocket, bringing 'em home. Julian found one, swiped it. But he didn't hurt that girl, didn't wanna hurt her. I think Julian... He liked her. A crush. Just trying to show off for her or something. Being stupid. Being a boy. Not like he punched her, watched her bleed all over her perfect little pink outfit.

(Beat, **KATHLEEN** *watches* **JO** *carefully;* **JO** *purposely ignores her, and makes a note.)*

JO. When these violent episodes occurred, how did you handle it at home?

KATHLEEN. I talked to him. "You scared that little girl," I told him. "Girls don't like that. They don't play same way as boys." Julian never quite figured out girls.

JO. Was Harlan involved in the disciplinary process?

KATHLEEN. I had a job, too, you know.

JO. Yes, I know.

KATHLEEN. Just saying that Harlan wasn't the only one working. I had a full-time job. Still have it. Paper mill. Night shift. So –

JO. Why night shift? Couldn't you –

KATHLEEN. Pays more.

JO. I see.

(She makes a quick note.)

If I may, Harlan was a good provider, no doubt. Why then did you need to work so much? Wasn't his income –

KATHLEEN. Jesus, there's a rich people question for you.

JO. I'm sorry. Um…let me back up. We –

KATHLEEN. I was working all night, sleeping all day. I couldn't always be there every time something went wrong. And Harlan, he was Julian's father. So yes, he… I mean, he had to do his share of the parenting, right?

JO. What did Harlan's share of the parenting consist of?

(Short beat.)

JO. Kathleen, what did –

KATHLEEN. Harlan tried his best to discipline Julian.

JO. By doing what?

KATHLEEN. Whatever was called for.

JO. For example?

KATHLEEN. He scolded him or…or grounded him.

JO. Physically, did he –

KATHLEEN. Just 'cause you don't spank your little boy, doesn't make it wrong.

JO. Aside from spanking, were there other physical punish–

KATHLEEN. I was working! I couldn't always be there. OK? I couldn't… And the fighting stopped. That little girl, that was the last time Julian ever –

(Short beat.)

Fighting stopped. Unless you got some piece of paper that says different.

JO. I do not, but I –

KATHLEEN. Ask me about something else.

JO. Something else? What do you –

KATHLEEN. I'm tired of talking about this. Ask me something else.

> *(**JO** puts aside the paper she is working from, pulls out another.)*

JO. When did Julian get his first gun?

KATHLEEN. Why?

> *(**JO** waits her out.)*

His twelfth birthday. Harlan bought Julian a pistol, a .22. Julian getting a gun, that was a good thing.

JO. How so?

KATHLEEN. 'Cause for the first time ever, the two of them actually started spending time together. Going to the gun club, looking things up online and talking, really talking about... Why isn't that a good thing? And Harlan taught Julian the right and proper way to use a gun. He was very strict about it. Maintenance and cleaning the gun and storing ammunition and...and safety! Treat every gun as if it's loaded. Never point your gun at anything unless you intend to –

> *(Agitated, she stops herself.* **JO** *watches her carefully.)*

But most important, they were getting along. Julian and Harlan, just like a boy and his dad, like I always wanted for him.

JO. I see.

> *(She makes a note.)*

Did you ever worry that –

KATHLEEN. That's all I have to say about guns. Ask me something else.

> *(***JO*** *puts aside the paper she was working from, pulls out another, reads it silently for a moment.)*

JO. Did you read the coroner's report on Julian?

KATHLEEN. Cause of death, bullet to the brain. That's all I needed to know.

JO. So, you never read the full report?

KATHLEEN. No.

JO. How did Julian break his fingers?

KATHLEEN. What?

JO. According to the report, three fingers on Julian's left hand had been broken approximately three or four years prior to his death. Julian would have been thirteen or –

KATHLEEN. I remember.

JO. So, how did he break his fingers?

KATHLEEN. Um...he was helping Harlan do something with the car and... I don't remember exactly.

JO. The car? So, you weren't there when it happened?

KATHLEEN. No.

JO. Can you tell me why the fingers weren't set properly?

KATHLEEN. What do you mean?

JO. According to the report, the fingers were never set properly by a doctor and so –

KATHLEEN. How can they tell that? See, I don't trust those police.

JO. This was the coroner's report.

KATHLEEN. I don't trust any of 'em. They're all just trying to make it look like Julian... And how can the coroner...after he's dead, how can he go back and... I don't believe it.

JO. The report clearly states that the fingers were not –

KATHLEEN. Besides, we took him to the hospital.

JO. Oh. So, they did set his fingers. Then why –

KATHLEEN. Well, I mean... Harlan took him to the hospital.

JO. Oh.

KATHLEEN. I couldn't go because...work, probably. So, Harlan took him.

JO. I see. So, when Julian returned from the hospital, was he –

KATHLEEN. He had, you know…bandages. All that.

JO. Bandages, of course. Was he in a lot of pain?

KATHLEEN. He broke his fingers, yeah, he was in pain.

JO. Was he given a prescription for painkillers?

KATHLEEN. I don't remember. Look, I know what you're doing, trying to make this all about Harlan, but –

JO. No, I –

KATHLEEN. – it is not Harlan's fault if the doctor didn't do his job.

JO. Agreed, Kathleen, but –

KATHLEEN. Ah, but that won't do for your book. Gotta be abuse if it's gonna make it in the –

JO. I am not claiming abuse –

KATHLEEN. Fuzzword!

JO. I'm not! But you weren't there when Julian broke his fingers, you didn't go to the hospital, so I wonder –

KATHLEEN. I was working. Night shift! You have any idea what it's like to work at – no, of course not, stupid question.

JO. Kathleen, I am not criticizing you –

KATHLEEN. Yeah, you keep saying that.

JO. I am simply raising the possibility that Harlan may have –

KATHLEEN. You think it's so goddamn easy?! After what your little boy did to that girl, how can you –

JO. Leave Jake out –

KATHLEEN. – criticize me or Harlan or –

JO. I am not criticiz–

KATHLEEN. You don't spank your little boy. Truth is, you're afraid to even go near him.

JO. I refuse to let my son be part of this // conversation –

KATHLEEN. // How d'you know your husband doesn't spank him // when you're out on your book tours –

JO. // Kathleen, that's enough!

KATHLEEN. He could be smacking your boy around right now. Sounds like the little shit could use –

JO. Stop!

KATHLEEN. Oh, forgot. You don't hit him, just grab him and shake!

JO. Stop it!!!

KATHLEEN. My son is innocent! He is a victim, same as all the others. So, whether Harlan broke his fingers – which he didn't – or abu– ...did stuff to him or not, it doesn't matter! My son did not kill those people! He was a good boy! Nobody knew him like I did! Nobody!!!

> (**KATHLEEN** *sits back in the chair, spent, hand covering her eyes.* **JO** *crosses away. Silence.*)

JO. I need...

> (*She tries unsuccessfully to take a deep breath.*)

I need some fresh air.

> (*She crosses to a window. Another deep breath.*)

Let's, um... Let's take a break, and then –

KATHLEEN. I'm done for the day.

JO. No. We need a break, for sure, but –

KATHLEEN. I'm done for the day. Come back in the morning.

JO. Kathleen, we're behind. We've wasted far too much time –

KATHLEEN. And when you do come back, know what we're gonna talk about? Why Julian didn't do it. Gonna talk about all the evidence that Alan told me. And you will see, once and for all, that –

JO. I think it's an excellent idea. We can… We can work together to review everything Covington told you. But let's do it now, today, instead of wasting the entire afternoon –

KATHLEEN. I'm done for the day!

JO. Fine.

> (**JO** *starts to pack her things.*)

But there is still a lot to cover. We may have to extend the interview through Friday.

KATHLEEN. I gotta go back to work, starting Thursday night.

> (**JO** *sighs in frustration.*)

Already took off three nights for you. Can't afford to –

JO. *(Puts up a hand to stop her.)* OK.

> *(Short beat.)*

Kathleen, I'm just worried that –

KATHLEEN. And don't you need to get home to your little boy?

> (**JO** *is still for the slightest moment, then quickly finishes her packing. She looks at* **KATHLEEN** *with a tense, polite smile.*)

JO. I really did enjoy the stories about Julian. The Spring Fling story, that goes in the book, I promise.

(Beat.)

JO. Kathleen, I'm sorry about the way things played out today. I –

> *(**KATHLEEN** deliberately moves away from her. **JO** crosses to the door.)*

Get some rest.

> *(**JO** exits.)*

> *(**KATHLEEN** listens for **JO** to walk away. She walks into the kitchen, returns with a pen and a new set of index cards, still in their cellophane wrapper.)*

> *(**KATHLEEN** pulls out a cell phone and Covington's business card. She dials the number on the card, holds the phone to her ear and waits, tearing the cellophane from the index cards with her teeth as she does so.)*

> *(Blackout.)*

Scene Four

(The following morning, Wednesday, around 9:30.)

*(**KATHLEEN** has her stack of index cards and a few loose papers in front of her.)*

*(**JO** listens and takes notes.)*

*(Both **WOMEN** drink coffee.)*

KATHLEEN. OK. The gun.

JO. Which one?

KATHLEEN. The handgun that was on the floor.

JO. The Glock-19.

KATHLEEN. Right. Alan told me that if Julian had shot himself with it, then the gun would stay in his hand. It'd be impossible for him to drop it, 'cause after he pulled the trigger there'd be…um…

(She refers to an index card, reads.)

An involuntary response, that's it. The fingers would like…clutch, you know, they'd grip the gun and hold onto it. But the gun was found, like five, six feet away on the floor.

JO. True, but it's not uncommon –

KATHLEEN. You said you wouldn't interrupt me.

JO. I'm sorry. Please continue.

KATHLEEN. *(Checks her card.)* Plus, CNN said the gun was in Julian's hand, but it wasn't.

*(**KATHLEEN** picks up a new index card. **JO** writes in her notebook.)*

KATHLEEN. OK, Anthony Bova, the man, the carpenter, you know, who wandered into the alley during the shooting, remember him? CNN said he was one of –

JO. One of the shooters, yes, I remember.

KATHLEEN. Did you know he had a criminal record?

JO. No.

> (**KATHLEEN** *goes through her papers, takes one and posts it on a makeshift bulletin board – a wall, perhaps, or a cardboard box.*)

KATHLEEN. There. That's his mug shot.

> (**JO** *crosses to the picture, inspects it.*)

I never knew you could get stuff like this on the computer. Mug shots. Did you?

JO. Yes. How did you get this? You said you your computer died.

KATHLEEN. I went down to Mecklenburg Library.

JO. When?

KATHLEEN. Yesterday after you left. OK, so Bova was arrested three times for assault. Once for domestic... you know, hitting his wife. Twice for hitting...other people, I guess. The police didn't investigate him at all. They never even searched his workshop or his house. Seem weird to you?

> (**KATHLEEN** *picks up a new index card.*)

OK, so there's that. Then two of the guys who worked at the warehouse also had police records.

> (**KATHLEEN** *takes two sheets of paper, secures them next to the other one on the "bulletin board."*)

First, Michael McCoy. And Harlan didn't like Mike McCoy. Said he was lazy, late all the time. And I know that Mike McCoy owned guns 'cause he went to the same gun club Harlan and Julian did. So, here's someone that has a police record. Second, he has guns and, third, Harlan didn't like him.

> (**KATHLEEN** *sits back down, back to her index cards.*)

JO. What was Michael McCoy charged with?

KATHLEEN. He wasn't charged with anything. That's my –

JO. No, you said he had a police record, from before.

KATHLEEN. Oh. Um…

JO. *(Crosses to "bulletin board," reads.)* First time…assault, girlfriend. Second time…assault, girlfriend. Same charge, different women.

KATHLEEN. Welcome to Mecklenburg.

JO. How'd you find this website with the mug shots?

KATHLEEN. Alan gave me the address.

JO. Last week?

KATHLEEN. Mm-hm. OK, so that's Anthony Bova and Michael McCoy, two suspects the police never investigated. Now, another warehouse employee with a criminal record, Ricky Skiff.

> (*She posts a final sheet on the "bulletin board."*)

He was killed that day, but what I didn't know is that he died from a single gunshot wound to the head – same way Julian died. So –

JO. Forgive me, Kathleen –

KATHLEEN. What?

JO. That's incorrect. Richard Skiff died from multiple gunshot wounds.

> *(**JO** crosses back to her computer, searches for a document.)*

KATHLEEN. No. Alan said. Um...

> *(**KATHLEEN** checks her index card.)*

Single gunshot wound to the head, same as Julian. So, Alan thinks it's possible that Ricky committed suicide after he...you know, shot everybody.

> *(Having found what she wants, **JO** turns the computer screen to face **KATHLEEN**.)*

JO. Richard Skiff died from multiple wounds inflicted by the Remington ACR.

KATHLEEN. OK, so then he shot himself with the Remington.

JO. He couldn't have shot himself multiple times, no.

KATHLEEN. But Alan said –

JO. Alan is wrong.

> *(She refers to the computer.)*

See here? Richard Skiff. Wounds to the neck, back of the head, the torso. He could not have done that to himself. Right?

> *(**KATHLEEN** glares at her.)*

Plus, the Remington – registered to Harlan Kenney – was ultimately found strapped across Julian's back. Skiff's body was some seventy-five feet away in the workers' lounge. If Skiff had shot himself, wouldn't you expect the gun he used to be nearby?

KATHLEEN. Not if somebody moved it.

JO. Like who?

KATHLEEN. Like whoever was trying to make it look like Julian was the shooter.

(**JO** *bites her tongue, makes a quick note.*)

And here's the thing about Ricky Skiff – he was a criminal. He'd been in prison.

JO. Yes, I know all about Ricky Skiff.

KATHLEEN. He's on that…that list that they –

JO. Registered sex offenders.

KATHLEEN. But Alan says that after the shooting the police never even investigated him. So how can you trust the police and how can you trust that stupid report? Like the broken fingers. Jesus! Alan, he says there's no way the coroner could know all that about his fingers. He says –

JO. Wait. You discussed the coroner's report with Covington when he was here? Last week?

> (**KATHLEEN**, *avoiding* **JO**'s *gaze, examines her index card.*)

The same report that, yesterday, you told me you'd never read?

KATHLEEN. I haven't read it, but, um… I just asked Alan about the broken fingers and he said –

JO. Last week?

KATHLEEN. You're interrupting me again.

JO. I'm confused –

KATHLEEN. Just wait!

> (*She quickly sifts through her pile of cards and yanks one out.*)

OK, Emily Murdock –

JO. I'd like to clarify –

KATHLEEN. Emily Murdock!

JO. What about her?

KATHLEEN. OK. Geez.

(*A deep breath.*)

Emily...she has this reputation as being this really... OK, she was paralyzed. Which is real sad, don't get me... But everybody thinks she's so... But maybe she's not.

JO. Not what?

KATHLEEN. So perfect! Jesus. Nobody's willing to...to question anything she says and so if she says Harlan kicked Julian and that's why Julian shot... See, nobody's willing to doubt her. That's all I'm saying.

JO. And you're telling me there is reason to doubt Emily?

KATHLEEN. Alan says there are stories about her.

JO. Stories?

KATHLEEN. Stories that Emily was...um, sleeping with Ricky Skiff and that she...she posed for photos for him. You know...nude.

(**JO** *levels her gaze at* **KATHLEEN**.)

JO. Nude photos?

KATHLEEN. Yes.

JO. Nude photos? That's Covington's next...

(**JO** *shakes her head in disgust.*)

Why do these men have to sexualize everything? Turn it into –

KATHLEEN. I'm probably not explaining it right. See, Alan says –

JO. Stop. Just...stop!

*(Beat, **KATHLEEN** looking anxiously at **JO**.)*

OK, let's back up. First, it's quite common for a handgun used in a suicide to be found on the floor, or somewhere nearby – chair, lap, kitchen counter, wherever the –

KATHLEEN. How do you know that?

JO. Research. They conducted a study. Texas. The shooter drops the gun something like seventy-five percent of the time. So Covington's claim that –

KATHLEEN. I don't believe it. Alan said it was imposs–

JO. Second, at the time of the shooting, Anthony Bova was in the alley, Michael McCoy was sick at home. Neither man was in the warehouse, so in spite of their admittedly disturbing criminal histories, no reasonable person could –

KATHLEEN. But Alan says that –

JO. Alan is not a reasonable person, Kathleen, and he is wrong. Wrong about the gun, wrong about Ricky Skiff, wrong when he said my friend in Virginia had it coming!

KATHLEEN. Why are you getting so angry?

JO. Nude photos, seriously? Has Covington seen them? Have you?

KATHLEEN. Me, no. Alan, I don't... But it changes things.

*(**JO** barks out an angry laugh.)*

Your turn to listen to me now!

*(**JO** faces her.)*

It changes things. If Emily was with Ricky then that's... I mean, maybe that's why she's protecting him. Alan says –

JO. Protecting him how?

KATHLEEN. By saying Julian was the shooter!

JO. OK, let me make sure I understand. Emily Murdock, married mother of twin daughters, was sleeping with Richard Skiff, sexual predator, and she posed nude for him.

KATHLEEN. I'm not saying she definitely –

JO. Skiff went on a rampage, killing thirteen, shooting Emily in the back. Skiff then shoots himself – multiple times, I might add – and now Emily, paralyzed for life, is protecting the man who –

KATHLEEN. The police never even looked at Ricky Skiff's computer to see if –

JO. Kathleen, dear god!

KATHLEEN. – there was anything to connect him to the shooting and so if dirty pictures of Emily were on his computer, they –

JO. Emily Murdock did not pose for nude photos for Ricky Skiff!

KATHLEEN. How do you know?

JO. Because the painfully shy woman I spent three hours with yesterday afternoon –

KATHLEEN. You met her?

JO. You threw me out, Kathleen. I had to find a productive use for my –

KATHLEEN. I'm not allowed to talk to Alan but it's OK for you to –

JO. I was doing my job!

KATHLEEN. I'm your job!!! I'm the mother, goddammit, not that Murdock woman. I'm the mother and my boy didn't do it! My boy –

JO. Every living witness has identified Julian as –

KATHLEEN. Alan Covington knows all about you! He says that *Evil Men* book you wrote, it pissed off the family of the murdered woman 'cause it was so sympathetic to the killer. Family might even sue. Alan says you have a terrible reputation, and your publisher's pissed off at you and –

JO. And since you believe every ridiculous lie this man tells you, it must be true.

KATHLEEN. He knows all about you!

JO. I assume he told you this yesterday afternoon. When you called him, immediately after I left.

KATHLEEN. So what?

JO. After I specifically warned you against speaking with –

KATHLEEN. So what?! Alan told me all he had to do was snap his fingers and I'd have another book deal tomorrow. He even has a writer in mind, this woman who works for him and she'd write it from my point of view, with my opinions and my evidence and my truth!

JO. Get a good lawyer.

KATHLEEN. Oh, stop trying to scare me. I'll just give you the money back and we can –

JO. It's not that simple, Kathleen. It's not just the money we paid you, it's also the money we've invested in this project. Research, legal fees, travel. And, of course, damages for –

KATHLEEN. Damages? For what?

JO. Kathleen, when you violate a contract like –

KATHLEEN. Violate? How did I –

JO. By speaking with Covington! By –

KATHLEEN. Sue me! I don't care! You can't possibly do anything to me that will make my life any more miserable than it already is. I know that's what you want, but –

JO. That is not what I –

KATHLEEN. Since the moment you walked through that door, you've done nothing but...but criticize me and judge me –

JO. I do not judge –

KATHLEEN. You judge me every time you look at me! And who are you, anyway? What, 'cause you're famous and... *Josepha* and you got this book with...Shakespeare, you think you're some... But you're not.

(**JO** *laughs ironically, starts to walk away.*)

You're just a sad, pathetic woman, afraid to even touch her own little boy.

(**JO** *stops at this, turns to face* **KATHLEEN.**)

JO. So...you can see the truth when it suits you. Is that it, Kathleen?

(*A beat, and then* **JO** *starts to pack up her briefcase, continues to do so throughout the following.*)

KATHLEEN. What are you doing?

JO. First, I'm going to get something to eat. Not even ten a.m. but I could go for a Big Mac. Then I'm going to see Emily Murdock and –

KATHLEEN. Why?

JO. Well, if you're not going to work with me, I need to find a new angle for the book. I liked Emily and I'm sure she could use the money.

KATHLEEN. You mean you're still gonna write this book?

JO. Yes, of course.

KATHLEEN. No, you –

JO. That's not up to you, Kathleen.

> *(As she reaches around* **KATHLEEN** *to pick up a few items for the briefcase.)*

Excuse me.

KATHLEEN. You can't use anything I told you. About Julian or Harlan or...or Thanksgiving or –

JO. We'll see.

KATHLEEN. No, you can't!

JO. Oh, and you might tell Covington that I will take all necessary steps to protect Emily Murdock from his hateful insinuations about her relationship with Ricky –

KATHLEEN. Wait! You want to protect that Murdock woman –

JO. Yes! Kathleen, don't you see what Covington is doing by –

KATHLEEN. That woman lied about my boy! And what else is she hiding? What else –

JO. I will not allow you or Covington to victimize Emily further.

KATHLEEN. She is nothing but a –

JO. Her life was devastated by your son –

KATHLEEN. No!

JO. *(Continuous.)* – and now you want to drag her through the muck so you can preserve your pathetic lie.

KATHLEEN. It is not a –

JO. She has suffered enough!

KATHLEEN. What about me? I haven't suffered enough for you? Is that why you came here, to...to torture me, to... What about me?!!!

(**JO** *starts to speak.*)

You never once said you were sorry for my loss. I lost my son and my husband on the same goddamn day in the worst way possible, but nobody ever – nobody! Not even you. You say you want to be my friend, but, Jesus, you're just like everybody else, like all the... this goddamn town, I can't even... I go to the grocery store or work or even the library yesterday. People point. "There she is, the mother." And the phone calls, and people throwing rocks at the house, and leaving dead animals on the... Oh yeah, some asshole went to the trouble of killing thirteen rabbits and leaving the bloody bodies on my porch.

(**JO** *reacts audibly.*)

Even after I move outta the house, move in here, they just keep... Jesus, the letters, the packages, they just keep... You wanna see?

JO. Kathleen, no –

KATHLEEN. *(Moving to the closet.)* No, I think you need to see. I saved 'em for you. Thought they'd be good for the book.

(*She pulls out a shoebox containing a stack of loose papers. She grabs one off the top and reads it.*)

"Why didn't he kill you, too, you worthless cow?"

(*She tosses the letter at* **JO**, *pulls out another.*)

"Satan waits for you in the lake of fire and you shall be tormented day and night forever and ever."

(*She tosses the letter at* **JO**, *pulls out another.*)

Oh, here's a good one. Came yesterday.

JO. Kathleen, let's calm –

KATHLEEN. *(Reading.)* "How about I stick my .38 Special in your pussy and pull the trigger? Blow you in half, bitch."

    (**KATHLEEN** *tosses the letter at* **JO**.*)*

JO. Oh my god.

KATHLEEN. *(Reading one last letter.)* "You call yourself a mother?"

    (Her voice cracks on the word "mother." **JO** *rips the letter out of* **KATHLEEN**'s *hand, throws it aside.)*

JO. Oh, Kathleen, I'm sorry. That's enough, please –

KATHLEEN. He liked them. Bob and Sally. Why would he… If he liked them, why would he… Why?

JO. I don't know.

KATHLEEN. And he was happy, that last week, he was… I walked past his room and he was on his bed in the dark and I said, "Julian, are you awake?" "Yeah, Ma." So, I went in and…and he gave me the sweetest kiss and hugged me so tight, like when he was a baby. So tight. "Are you OK, sweetheart?" And he said, "Yeah, Ma, I'm good." But then the next morning, he –

    *(***KATHLEEN*** pushes* **JO** *away, lets out a scream of rage, and throws the stack of letters in her hand. They go flying. She tears the sheets of paper from the "bulletin board," flings them aside.)*

    *(***KATHLEEN*** goes on a rampage, swiping her hand at Jo's papers, swiping at Jo's laptop, flinging Jo's notebook aside.* **KATHLEEN** *loses her balance.)*

(*JO, who has backed off during the rampage, moves in quickly and catches* **KATHLEEN** *before she falls, lowers her awkwardly but gently to the floor.*)

JO. Shh, it's OK, it's OK. Shhhh.

(**KATHLEEN** *looks at* **JO**.)

KATHLEEN. He was happy, he... "Yeah, Ma, I'm good. I'm good."

(*Looking at* **JO** *and speaking plainly.*)

I don't know why he did it. Can you tell me why?

JO. No.

(**KATHLEEN** *emits a sob, collapsing in* **JO**'s *arms.*)

KATHLEEN. I loved him and I tucked him in and I held his hand when he crossed the street and I told him I loved him every day and I held him so tight, as tight as I could...and he got away from me. He got away...

(**KATHLEEN** *sobs,* **JO** *holding her.*)

Oh my god, all those people.

JO. Shhhh.

KATHLEEN. Those poor people. What did I do?

JO. Kathleen –

KATHLEEN. I let my boy down.

JO. Shhhh.

(**JO** *cradles* **KATHLEEN**, *rocking her as she sobs. Pause.*)

KATHLEEN. When you write the book, I want you to say that…say that Julian was happy those last days and I could never imagine… Can the book say that?

JO. Yes.

KATHLEEN. And it needs to say Julian was brave. Can the book say that he was brave?

JO. I promise.

KATHLEEN. 'Cause he wasn't scared at all. When I got to my mother's house, he was sitting, sweet and quiet. Hush, Mommy. The lady whispering hush. Hush, Mommy, hush…hush…hush…hussshhh…

*(**JO** holds **KATHLEEN**, rocking her gently.)*

End of Play